Puedes consultar nuestro catálogo en www.picarona.net

Las aventuras de Kandi: Kandi y el zorro
Texto: *Raynelda A. Calderón*
Ilustraciones: *Donna Wiscombe*

1.ª edición: noviembre de 2018

Título original: *Kandi's Adventures: Kandi and the Fox*

Maquetación: *Isabel Estrada*
Corrección: *Sara Moreno*

© 2018, Raynelda A. Calderón
(Reservados todos los derechos)

© 2018, Ediciones Obelisco, S. L.
www.edicionesobelisco.com
(Reservados los derechos para la lengua española)

Edita: Picarona, sello infantil de Ediciones Obelisco, S. L.
Collita, 23-25. Pol. Ind. Molí de la Bastida
08191 Rubí - Barcelona - España
Tel. 93 309 85 25 - Fax 93 309 85 23
E-mail: picarona@picarona.net

ISBN: 978-84-9145-203-4
Depósito Legal: B-25.453-2018

Printed in Spain

Impreso por ANMAN, Gràfiques del Vallès, S. L.
C/ Llobateres, 16-18, Tallers 7 - Nau 10, Polígon Industrial Santiga
08210 - Barberà del Vallès - Barcelona

Texto: **Raynelda A. Calderón**

Ilustraciones: **Donna Wiscombe**

Las aventuras de Kandi

Kandi y el Zorro

Kandi's Adventures

Kandi and the Fox

 Picarona

Ésta es Kandi, la ardilla voladora.
Las ardillas son más activas durante el día...,
pero Kandi es activa todo el día durante todo el año
porque le gusta volar y visitar diferentes lugares.

This is Kandi, the flying squirrel.
Squirrels are most active during the day...
but Kandi is active all day-long, all year-round.
She likes to fly a lot to visit different places.

Una calurosa tarde, Kandi fue a visitar
a su amiga Mika en el bosque,
y en el camino se encontró con ¡un zorro grandote!
Estaba tan asustada del zorro que se quedó congelada,
quietecita, pensando qué hacer para escapar.

One bright afternoon, Kandi went to visit
her friend Mika in the woods.
On her way, he came upon a big fox!
Kandi was very scared of the fox; she stood
quietly thinking about what to do to get away.

¡El zorro se estaba acercando a Kandi! Oh, no...
¿Qué podría hacer Kandi?
¿Gritar y asustar al zorro para que se fuera?
¿Pedir ayuda o pelear con ese gran zorro?

The fox was getting closer and closer! Oh, dear!
What should Kandi do?
Should she scream and scare the fox away?
Should she cry for help or fight?

Kandi corrió lo más rápido que pudo
al árbol más cercano y se escondió hasta
que el zorro, cansado de esperar, se fue.
¡Estuvo cerca!

Kandi ran very fast to the nearest tree
and hid there until the fox went away.
That was close!

Cuando Kandi llegó a casa de Mika, le contó su aventura
con el gran zorro y cómo se escondió en un árbol.
Mika se alegró mucho de ver que Kandi estaba sana
y salva y la felicitó por ser tan astuta y por su ingeniosa
idea de esconderse en el árbol.

When Kandi arrived to Mika's house, she told her all
about the fox and how she hid in the tree.
Mika was very happy to see that Kandi was alright
and congratulated her for being so brave
and for such a wise idea.

Mientras tomaban el té, Mika pensó que sería
una buena idea aprender acerca de los zorros
por si en el futuro se topaban con otro.
Juntas planearon un viaje a la biblioteca para buscar
un libro sobre los zorros y qué hacer frente al peligro.

As they had tea, Mika thought that it would be
a good idea if they learned about foxes in case
they came upon one again.
They planned a trip to the library to look for a book
about foxes and what to do when in danger.

Al día siguiente, Kandi y Mika se levantaron temprano,
tomaron el desayuno y fueron a la biblioteca.
¿Te gustaría venir a ti también?

The very next day, they got up early,
had breakfast and headed to the library.
Would you like to come too?

Habilidades de pensamiento crítico (ejemplos de preguntas e ideas)

- Mirando la cubierta, pregunta a los niños lo que saben sobre las ardillas.
- Pregunta a los niños qué saben sobre los zorros.
- Planea un viaje a la biblioteca como Kandi y Mika.
- ¿Qué clase de libros podemos encontrar en una biblioteca?
- ¿Has estado en una biblioteca? Si es así, describe lo que hiciste allí.
- Si quisieras aprender sobre los zorros y las ardillas, ¿sabes en qué sección de la biblioteca buscar esos libros?
- Pide a los niños que indiquen qué tipo de recursos podemos usar cuando necesitamos buscar información.
- Valores enseñados: coraje, resolución de problemas, pensamiento creativo.

Thinking Critically (sample questions and ideas)

- Looking at the cover, ask children what they know about squirrels.
- Ask children what they know about foxes.
- Plan a trip to the library like Kandi and Mika.
- What kind of books can we find in a library?
- Have you even been to a library? If so, describe what you did there.
- If you wanted to learn about foxes and squirrels, in what section of the library will you look for those books?
- Ask children to name what type of resources we can use when we need to look for information.
- Teaching values: courage, problem solving, creative thinking.

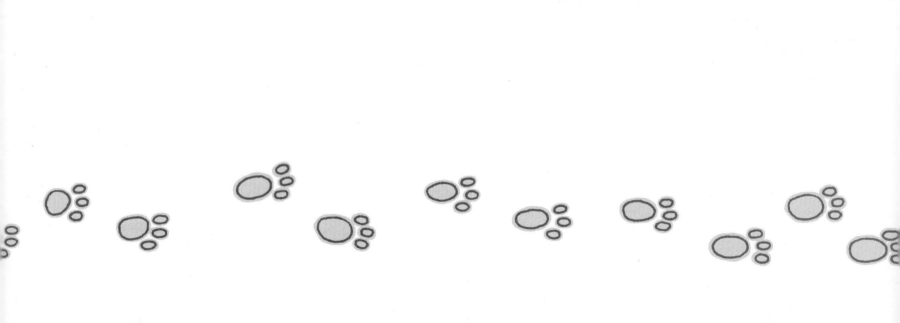

MISS MEOW

Jane Smith

WEST
MARGIN
PRESS

For my mom, Cheryl, and our cats,
Tiger and Socks, with lots and lots of love!

Library of Congress Cataloging-in-Publication Data

Names: Smith, Jane, 1978- author, illustrator.
Title: Miss Meow / Jane Smith.
Description: Berkeley : West Margin Press, [2021] | Audience: Ages 4-8. | Audience: Grades K-1. | Summary: Dressed in cat ears and a tail, Miss Meow blames her little brother for destroying her favorite toy, but after further investigation she discovers she might not be the only cat in the house.
Identifiers: LCCN 2021013957 (print) | LCCN 2021013958 (ebook) | ISBN 9781513289458 (hardback) | ISBN 9781513289465 (ebook)
Subjects: CYAC: Cats–Fiction. | Costume–Fiction. | Imagination–Fiction.
Classification: LCC PZ7.S64968 Mi 2021 (print) | LCC PZ7.S64968 (ebook) | DDC [E]--dc23
LC record available at https://lccn.loc.gov/2021013957
LC ebook record available at https://lccn.loc.gov/2021013958

Proudly distributed by Ingram Publisher Services

Printed in China
25 24 23 22 21 1 2 3 4 5

Published by West Margin Press®

WEST MARGIN PRESS

WestMarginPress.com

WEST MARGIN PRESS
Publishing Director: Jennifer Newens
Marketing Manager: Alice Wertheimer
Project Specialist: Micaela Clark
Editor: Olivia Ngai
Design & Production: Rachel Lopez Metzger
Design Intern: Evie Jones

Meow!!

(That's cat for "hello.")
This is Miss Meow. She's a cat.

Miss Meow loves to cuddle. If you pet her between her ears, she will purr really loud.

She's an expert hunter. She chases her mouse. Miss Meow is very fast.

She refuses to take a bath.
She'd rather lick herself clean.

Miss Meow
hates being wet!

She loves napping in the sunshine on her pillow bed. It smells like her and her smell warns intruders to stay away.

She laps water from her water dish and nibbles cheese crackers from her food bowl.

If anyone even thinks about stealing her snacks, Miss Meow hisses at them.

She scratches anyone who pulls her tail, even if it is her little brother, Felix. And it's *always* Felix.

HiSS!

Miss Meow is territorial.
She chases off intruders and
protects all her favorite things.

What happened to Miss Meow's mouse?!

Miss Meow's fur stands straight up. Her ears flatten against her head. She knows who did this—who *always* does this!

Miss Meow stalks toward her brother, pointing her claw. Miss Meow's food bowl has been knocked over.

Cheese crackers are scattered across the floor.

CRUNCH!

"Grrr!" she growls. "Look what you did now!
My snack is ruined!"

Mom picks up Felix.
"What's going on, Miss Meow?"
she asks.

Miss Meow *howls* in frustration and scratches at the floor with her foot.

Whoops! She slips on a wet patch.

Miss Meow lands *hard* on all fours.

Meee-OW!

Felix wiggles down.
"Look!" he calls out.

A mysterious trail of wet paw prints paces across the kitchen floor.

Miss Meow springs to her feet and prowls down the hall. The paw prints disappear into her room. Miss Meow peeks inside.

There's a sopping-wet *intruder* sleeping on her pillow bed!

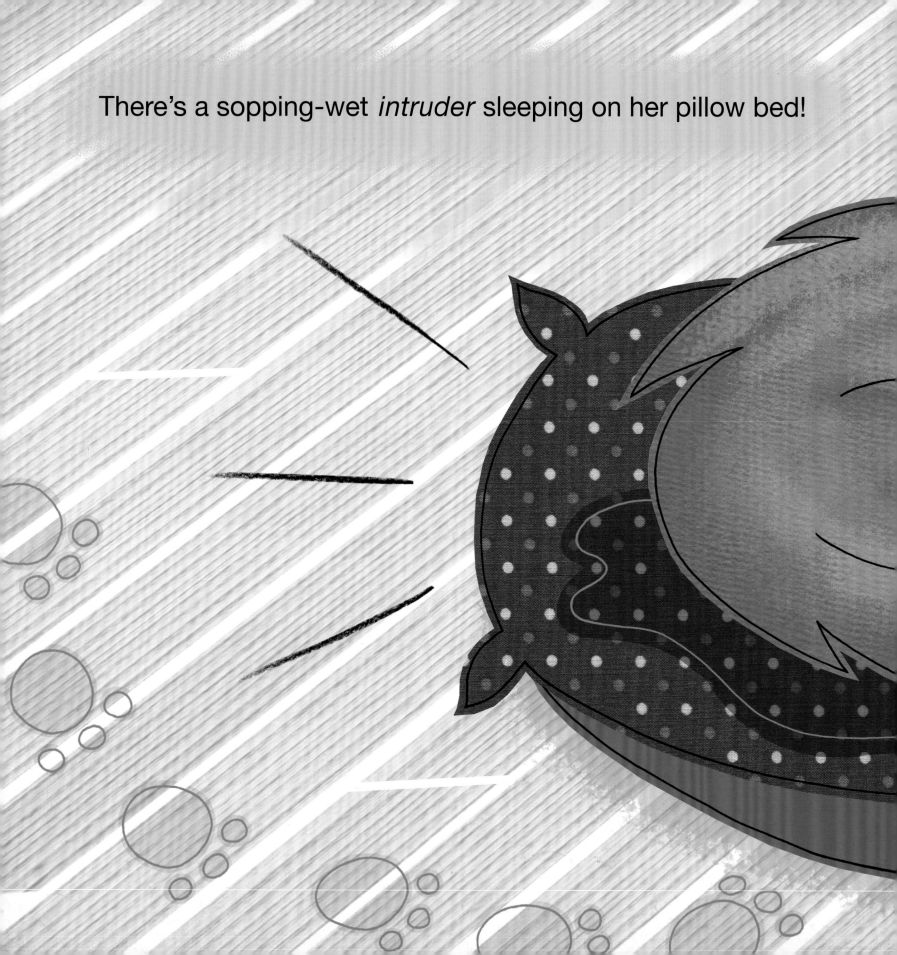

"Two Miss Meows!" Felix shrieks with delight. Startled, the soggy stray cat lifts his head and freezes.

Whoosh!

Quick as a lightning flash,
the stray cat streaks out the door.

That mouse-destroying, snack-spilling,
bed-ruining bugaboo, thinks Miss Meow.

"Come back here!" she caterwauls as she chases after him.

They bolt through the living room.

They race across the playroom.

They dart around and around the dining room, until...

Screeech!

They skid to a stop in the kitchen. Miss Meow has him cornered! The stray cat claws at the window, desperate to escape. "Meee-yowl!" he wails.

Miss Meow's heart softens. The stray cat is shivering. He hates being wet too!

"Here, kitty. It's okay," she coos softly. Miss Meow holds out her hand to show she is friendly.

Felix crawls up next to Miss Meow.
"I'm sorry, Felix," Miss Meow whispers.
Felix purrs.

The stray cat approaches cautiously and sniffs.

Then he rubs his head under her hand.
Miss Meow pets him between his ears.
He purrs really loud.

Suddenly, the cat snatches up her mouse. Felix and Miss Meow giggle as fluff flies everywhere.

It turns out the territory in Miss Meow's heart is bigger than she thought.

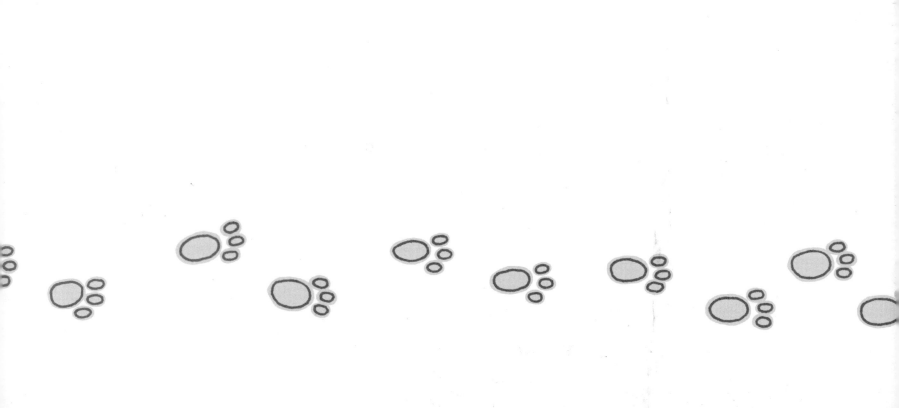